Lea and the Bird Feeder

written by Jay Dale
illustrated by Amanda Gulliver

"Dad!" said Lea.

"I can see lots of birds."

"Yes," said Dad.

"The birds are looking for food."

"Can we make a bird feeder for the birds?" said Lea.

"Not today," said Dad. "I have to dig the garden."

Lea looked sad.
"The birds are **very** hungry,"
she said.

Dad looked at Lea.

Then he looked at the birds.

“Come on,” he said.

“Let’s make a bird feeder.”

Dad and Lea went into the shed.
Dad got two bits of wood.
He cut the wood into little bits.

Lea got a new box of nails.
Then she got an old hammer.

Lea hit the nails into the wood.

Bang! Bang! Bang!

"This bird feeder looks good," said Lea.

"Yes," said Dad. "I like the roof on the top. It's good to have a roof on a bird feeder."

Lea got a new box of seed. The seed went into the bird feeder.

At last, Dad and Lea went outside.

“Where will the bird feeder go?” said Lea.

“It can go in this big tree,” said Dad.

"Look at the birds!" cried Lea.
"They are eating the seed.
This bird feeder is the best!"